SCHOLASTIC Phonics

Up at Night

Published in the UK by Scholastic Education, 2022
Scholastic Distribution Centre, Bosworth Avenue, Tournament Fields, Warwick, CV34 6UQ
Scholastic Ireland, 89E Lagan Road, Dublin Industrial Estate, Glasnevin, Dublin, D11 HP5F

SCHOLASTIC and associated logos are trademarks and/or registered trademarks of Scholastic Inc.
www.scholastic.co.uk
© 2022 Scholastic
2 3 4 5 6 7 8 9   4 5 6 7 8 9 0 1 2 3

Printed by Ashford Colour Press
The book is made of materials from well-managed, FSC-certified forests and other controlled sources.

A CIP catalogue record for this book is available from the British Library.

ISBN 978-0702-30896-3

All rights reserved. This book is sold subject to the condition that it shall not, by way of trade or otherwise, be lent, hired out or otherwise circulated in any form of binding or cover other than that in which it is published. No part of this publication may be reproduced, stored in a retrieval system, or transmitted in any form or by any other means (electronic, mechanical, photocopying, recording or otherwise) without prior written permission of Scholastic Limited.

Every effort has been made to trace copyright holders for the works reproduced in this publication, and the publishers apologise for any inadvertent omissions.

Author
Charlotte Raby
Editorial team
Rachel Morgan, Vicki Yates, Tracy Kewley, Jennie Clifford
Design team
Dipa Mistry, Justin Hoffmann, Andrea Lewis, We Are Grace
Illustrations
Becky Down/The Bright Agency

Help your child to read!

This book practises these letters and letter sounds.
Point and say the sounds with your child:

- ee
- igh
- oo (as in 'look')
- oo (as in 'food')

Your child may need help to read these common tricky words:

- we
- put
- and
- go
- the
- are
- full
- of
- I
- into
- they
- to
- be

Before reading
- Look at the cover picture and read the title together. Read the back cover blurb to your child.
- Ask your child: *Do you remember being outside at night? What did you do?*

During reading
- If your child gets stuck on a word, remind them to sound it out and then blend the sounds to read the word: f-oo-d, food.
- If they are still stuck, show them how to read the word.
- Enjoy looking at the pictures together. Pause to talk about the story.

After reading
- Ask your child: *What food would you like to eat from a food van?*
- *Have you ever seen an animal at night?*

Can you spot the duck on 6 pages?

It is night.

We put on coats and go.

We get a big bag of food.

Then we see its cubs.

They are a fantastic sight!

Retell the story